THE BOOKSELLER

THE BOOKSELLER

STORIES

PETER BRISCOE

PALO VERDE PRESS

This is a work of fiction. Names, characters, places, and incidents either are the product of the author's imagination or are used fictitiously. Any resemblance to actual persons, living or dead, events, or locales is entirely coincidental.

Published by Palo Verde Press

18608 Oak Park Drive

Riverside, California 92504

Cover designed by Nanne of 99designs

Library of Congress Control Number: 2020925573

ISBN 978-0-9634898-9-0

eISBN 978-0-9634898-5-2

To my daughter Adriana

CONTENTS

ONE OF OUR STARS

When I knew him he was starting to get a beer belly. It was easy to see because of the way he dressed: t-shirt, jeans, sandals. In winter he'd slip on a green tweed coat from his Yale days. He had a light-brown beard and fine blue eyes. The eyes got to a lot of women. One secretary in the department was so taken by him that she showed up at work in a miniskirt with nothing underneath, and bent over to pick up a crumpled piece of paper right in front of him. I swear this is true. He took her home and serviced her like a bull, but it came to nothing. He wasn't one to actually live with women. They take too much time, and what he set himself to learn, in six languages, took all of his. At the university they just let him do his thing.

Everyone agreed he was brilliant, and his publications were impeccable. Nor did they ask him to sit on committees, figuring he would rarely attend. Half the time he was on the other side of the world, in a jungle. It was easier to reach him there.

A GIRL IN COLOMBIA

Down the road, through a corridor of high trees, you could see her step off a bus that stopped where the road intersects the highway. She began slowly ascending. She was wearing a dress and sandals, and had a backpack. She seemed tired. She was the right age to be a college student, rather petite, with short brown hair. Her dress was a kind of hiker's sundress made out of rough tan cloth. When she got to the gatehouse of the park, where we were standing in line to buy entrance tickets, she took off the backpack, set it on the ground, and stooped over to fish out her money and passport. Her dress had a very wide collar, and when she bowed to rummage in her pack, it fell open revealing her breasts, which were beautiful. No bra, and I would suspect no underwear at all. I felt confused because she was not a sexy type. Almost the opposite. Demure, quiet-looking, pretty. After she found her documents, she got into a second line across from me. I noticed her legs, which were nice, and because the dress was sleeveless with large armholes, there were her breasts again, now in side view, firm, tanned, swelling. She was a lovely, young woman. Just as nature made her.

Immediately I thought: what is she doing here alone in this jungle park? Girls almost always travel in pairs or in groups for safety. This place had no rangers, poor signage, primitive trails, minimum facilities, and its share of unsavory types. Robberies on the trail were known to happen. What was this girl doing here by herself? I looked at her again. She had an air of class. I guessed that she came from a family of comfortable means and studied at the university. It was vacation time. Maybe she wanted to go backpacking, but couldn't interest her friends, so she left by herself. Not afraid. What an interesting woman. I wanted to know her. Not possible.

Que Dios la proteja.

AFTER YOU, PLEASE

It was depressing to realize that the older he got the less he knew. Wasn't it supposed to be the other way around? Doubly depressing because he made his living as a scholar. Oh, he could still shotgun blast an opponent with erudition and silence him, but he didn't believe a word of it. What he said was mostly for suckers.

Your students included? he asked himself.

Silence.

So what *do* you believe?

That good cooking is not only worthwhile, it is an accessible art. That a blow job is an old man's delight. That . . . There were a couple of others, but he couldn't remember them.

It strikes me you're not quite as lost as you allege.

Oh yeah?

A successful cousin had invited them to a 50th wedding anniversary, and he didn't want to go. The invitation specified formal attire (black tie optional). He would need to buy a new suit, and that would be the one they would bury him in. How could he enjoy wearing it? Instead of fine feathers, it would feel like a shroud.

Was he in poor health? No, merely getting creaky. But he no longer dressed up. Not since he retired (a word he detested). Now he was strictly blue collar. His wife said he looked like a woodchopper.

But his wife insisted they were going. Five years before she had bought a lovely gown anticipating a reception that would announce the engagement of their daughter. One way or another she was going to wear that gown.

Even the French didn't have a better word for it, though the Spanish did. *Jubilación*. To rejoice. What a prisoner might cry when set free. He considered alternatives:

Aisé.

A man of independent means.

A man of leisure. Awakening each morning . . . free. With the leisure old Greeks had. Maybe—except that he didn't own a slave. Not even a domestic.

Everyone asked him: How are you doing? *What* are you doing? All of them wondering if they would go crazy when their time came. Of course the only acceptable answer was: Fabulous! Just returned from a trip to Nepal; raised a million for my church's new grand organ; volunteer firefighter; museum docent; putting the finishing touches to a novel. Writing was always acceptable, indeed expected. Writing, writing. But he was sick of this pretentious BS. He merely said: I'm enjoying doing nothing. If I get bored, I'll take a job as a pizza delivery man.

But it wasn't quite true that he was doing nothing. He had inventoried a multitude of back-burner chores, projects, obligations, repairs. The garage, for instance, was stuffed to the rafters with all sorts of junk he had not had time to deal with during his busy career. Things were just thrown into it, leaving no room for automobiles. He did not want his daughter to have to confront this mess after he was dead. He knew his wife wouldn't touch it.

He figured he had eight extra hours per day compared to a working stiff. It should be easy to get a lot done. But when he threw himself into chores, he made little headway. His to-do list merely grew longer. He felt more and more inadequate, until he realized that a full-time job provides the perfect excuse for not getting much else done. Guilt can be shrugged off. The retiree, on the other hand, has no such excuse. He has lost his defense.

When you die, some believe you will finally see the face of God. But what he wanted to see was family and friends. To be reunited first with his schizophrenic son (healed) who would be waiting for him, *since the last shall be first*. Then with his wife, his daughter, his father and mother, his brother, his best friend, and so on. They would embrace, look into each other's eyes, sit, and hold hands. Too bad he didn't believe in an afterlife.

He was sitting in a waiting room, daydreaming. A woman entered and sat down next to him, quite close. She was attractive, and it became apparent that she wanted to stay near him. This was unusual, and he enjoyed the feeling. Being wanted, being chosen by this attractive dark-haired woman, made him feel very content—even as he realized who she was.

Although time was running out, he felt he didn't have to hurry. He was retired, after all. He could afford to let others go ahead of him.

THE BOOKSELLER

El Librero

Alfonso

A man is flying somewhere and reading a book. This is his way of life. He is a bookseller, on his way to buy, on his way to sell. He travels in more than one space and in more than one time. In many dimensions. He travels alone, but knows people in far-off places. They always welcome him, for business and for his company. They want to know where he's been, they want to hear new stories, and they want, of course, to see the rare and beautiful books he carries.

Yet he is not a naturally talkative person. Always courteous, yes. And knowledgeable. But quiet, reserved, watchful, full of secrets, of things he won't say. It is fruitless to ask him where he has found a book. Provenance is important in scholarship, but he will never divulge a source. Of course like any human being he loosens up at dinner when food and wine stretch the hours of the night. Then he may tell you how in Haiti just before the riots . . .

Or, on another night, a story like this . . .

"HE'S AT IT AGAIN. Old fool. Come on, let's have some fun."

The two page boys—they were still called that although they had been working in the library for years—walked over to the table where the man was standing up so he could wave to the proctor at the front of the reading room. His face was red, sweaty, and twitching. He wore metal-rimmed glasses which enlarged his eyes. He was going bald but still had a lot of curly hair on the sides. He was about sixty. As they approached they could hear him muttering.

"Señor Molina, is something wrong?"

"You are wrong. The books are wrong. The library. Something is very wrong."

"And just what is that, Señor? Tell us."

"You know perfectly well."

A third boy arrived pushing a cart which had one book on it. He handed it to the man, and said the others couldn't be found.

He glanced at the cover. "The least important book! You are wasting my time. This happened yesterday and the day before and last week. I wait an hour, and this is all I get? Why can't you find my books? Where are they? Who has them?"

"Mis-shelved, Señor. We are finding more and more like that."

"No you aren't 'finding' them. You're losing them. You are all imbeciles."

"Now, now, Señor, no shouting in the library. Besides the books you ask for are unusual, quite old."

"Why should that matter?"

"Perhaps they are worn out."

"Imbeciles!"

By now everyone in the room was staring. The man threw up his arms, gathered his papers and pens, stuffed them in his briefcase, and headed toward the exit. In leaving he did not address the proctor who sat at an elevated station, but merely glared at him. More than once he had complained to this stone about the incompetence of the staff and the disorder of the library.

THE ANCESTRY of this library began when the Jesuits were expelled from Spanish territories in 1767. It was a surprise military operation ordered by King Carlos III which took place throughout the continent on the same morning. The priests were rounded up and forced marched to ships awaiting at the ports, sometimes hundreds of kilometers away. Those who survived were transported to the Vatican. What they left behind were churches, colleges, schools, libraries, workshops, and vast mission plantations—in general superbly cared for and run. The best schools in America were Jesuit schools, and the best libraries as well. Fortunately (if such a word can be used after a depredation) some of these confiscated book collections became the nucleus of new libraries. Which was the case for La Biblioteca Pública de Carmona, Ecuador, founded in 1863. Still one of the grand post-independence buildings of the city.

The morning was sunny and rapidly warming up, the sky bright blue, as a man in a tan suit passed through the portal, pausing to let his eyes adjust to the dimmer light of the domed atrium. It was cool and quite comfortable, though the air was still and smelled—what? of old books? Some might say 'musty' but he rejected the word. He liked books.

To his left was a reception desk, in front an imposing staircase, and to the right an exhibit of early printing. In between these, tall arched doorways led to reading rooms. He told the receptionist that he was an inspector of police named Guillermo Robles, and would like to see the person who was in charge of the collection. They phoned Doctor Andrés Vidal who was in his office on the floor above. A library guard was asked to take him there.

After greetings and introductions were made, the inspector said: "We have had an odd complaint. It's probably nothing, but I thought I should bring it to your attention. The complainant states that there is rampant theft occurring in the library and that books of great value are missing."

"I'm sure that some are missing, but that is the case in all libraries. It's impossible to control at one hundred percent unless all users and even staff were barred from entry, and then you would no longer have a library, just a warehouse."

"So you are saying this isn't a problem?"

"Theft is always a problem. A universal problem. I can show you a list of books we are looking for, a very long list."

"Why so many?"

"This is an ancient library."

"Do you know Señor Gregorio Molina?"

"I have never had the pleasure."

"Perhaps you know his younger brother, Diputado Lorenzo Molina, now a candidate for prefect of the province."

"I see."

"The complainant is an unusual man, somewhat difficult, an eccentric who lives by himself in one of the rundown mansions of the family. He has never worked, but they say he is a scholar."

"I certainly wish Señor Molina had come to me first."

"And what would you have said to him, what would you have done?"

"Well, I would have discovered his research interests, and asked him what specific books he most needed. We could then launch a thorough search of the stacks, and if that proved unsuccessful we could try to find replacements by alerting the booktrade."

"You are a scholar yourself, aren't you, Doctor Vidal?"

"Yes, I still teach part-time at the university. My background is in philosophy, intellectual history, literature."

"Thus, the perfect librarian."

"There have only been one or two of those in history. I'm not there yet."

"Nonetheless, I'm sure our city is lucky to have you. Please send me a copy of the list of missing books."

Dr. Vidal sat in thought for a few moments, then phoned the director, Licenciado Rudolfo Gil.

"I have just had a visit from a police officer. He

came by because apparently a patron has complained about widespread book theft."

"And just why did he come to see you instead of me?"

"I have no idea. Perhaps because I am director of collections. Would you like to see him?"

"Not really. I think this is your problem. The important thing is for you to settle it quickly."

AFTER WORK DOCTOR VIDAL left the library and walked uphill to the university district and to a small restaurant he frequented. The owner was friendly, the food was good, and prior to the dinner hour it was peaceful. He sat down at a table against a wall and ordered a *chilcano de pisco*. Half an hour later an attractive, dark-haired woman entered, she waved, and he rose to greet and seat her at the table. Noticing that his tall glass was empty, she asked if he had had a hard day.

"Not the best. How was yours?"

"Nice. I have good students this term. And, fortunately, I do not have a boss like yours."

"Indeed. What would you like to drink?"

"I think an *albariño*. So what happened?"

He motioned the waiter over and ordered two glasses of wine.

"Not to make too much of it, but I had an unusual visitor today. A policeman, or rather a detective."

"He asked you to forgive his overdue fines?"

"As a matter of fact, this policeman does like to read. He was following up on a complaint that there's a lot of theft in the library."

"That's ridiculous! With all the violence and crime going on in this city, he spends his time on this?"

"It beats being shot at."

"Well, is there theft?"

"Of course, a lot. It happens in all libraries. It's hard to control. To stop theft you would have to bar users. In addition, you would have to staff the building with robots rather than human beings, to prevent the inside job. Do you know how little we pay the staff? To survive most of them have second jobs, including, for a few, selling our books."

"Do you know that for sure?"

"It's a guess."

"Well, what do you plan to do about it?"

"Now you're sounding like my boss."

"I mean, can you do anything?"

"I don't know."

They ordered dinner and changed the subject.

When it was time to go, he asked if she would like to drop by his place.

"Not tonight. I have papers to grade."

DR. VIDAL RETURNED HOME and decided that since Teresa couldn't join him he might as well work on a lecture he had agreed to give at the university. The topic was the Library as Idea. It appealed to him but also made him uneasy. Outwardly, to some observers, he was just a bureaucrat who assisted the director when he presented budget proposals to the alcalde's office. Others considered him the library's principal scholar, with a doctorate in philosophy and a knowledge of several languages. Once a year he taught a course in bibliography at the university, which students found surprising rigorous. He insisted it was the key to learning and to limitless knowledge. To staff he was courteous, greeting them with a smile and by name in the morning before disappearing into his office.

Coming to work, such an ordinary act, yet for Vidal, deep in his mind, it seemed a sacred act. That was the sort of feeling he would would never admit to anyone. They would think he was loco. Yet he entered the library as others enter a church. Indeed, there were times when passing through its great street doors, he shivered, not with fear but antic-ipation.

Such feelings made it difficult to write the lecture. He would have to translate emotion and subjectivity into an abstract, academic exposition. That got him thinking about a startling meeting he had had at the beginning of his career with the director of a U.S. library. The man had been a big shot automation expert at Stanford, which propelled him to the top job at another research library. At lunch he said: "Whenever I interview applicants, I always get around to asking them what things they personally enjoy doing. I'm listening for the words 'I love to read,' at which point I immediately cross them off the list. The last person you should ever hire in a library is someone like that."

"But *why*? I don't understand."

"Because things have changed, my friend. The modern library is not about knowledge as contained in books, but information retrieval, which is so much more efficient. The problem is not epistemological, it's inventory control. I know it's complicated, but, as a future administrator, you'll be all right if you just remember this: that a librarian reading a book is quite the same as a doctor screwing a patient. I leave that as my pearl for you."

Vidal paused and said to himself: Try imagining this man in the audience when you lecture. It will help you tone down the purple prose.

Although he had always been smart and a good student, he grew up in a small town that had neither a bookstore nor a library, normal for Latin America. His mother and father read the daily newspaper, subscribed to a ladies' magazine and a men's magazine, and ordered a few books by mail, including some for the children. But it was nowhere near enough for their thirsty boy. Like Cervantes he chased scraps of paper blowing in the street. Starting with his teachers he begged and borrowed unashamedly, and figured he had read every book in town by the time he applied for and won a scholarship to an American university. What a pleasure it was for his parents to read about *that* in the newspaper!

Arriving on campus a week early, he checked into the dormitory, settled into his room, and then took a walk about. It was twilight. What he noticed first were the vast lawns, being sprinkled. Then the famous schools, the laboratories, the auditoriums, still mostly empty and unlit. Far down the quad there was an enormous building that was lit up and he walked toward it. Soon, through every window, he saw books, row upon row of them. Obviously the library. It was open, so he entered that cool, luminous world, manned that night by a single person, a student employee reading a book, who smiled and swept his arm out in greeting. Not caring where he was going but very much wanting to take a long walk in a forest of books Vidal set out. Down one row then back another, looking, lingering, occasionally pulling out a volume to examine, as if he were picking a flower to smell. What truly awed him were the multi-volume sets, some hundreds of volumes long, beautifully bound, and written in numerous languages. One set, in Danish, astonished him. Because it was in Danish! Not a language that many people studied. The library seemed to have no limits. The only limit was a reader's desire and determination. It was thrilling and at the same time humbling.

He rarely expressed these feelings. So many people, even in the U.S., take libraries for granted. They are seen simply as buildings with lots of books in them, confusing to use, where old maids who run them tell people to keep quiet. Everybody, even nonreaders, think they know quite enough about libraries.

Something simple? Hardly. In reality the library is a space-time machine, where a reader can go anywhere, microscopically, telescopically, past, present and future, and especially into the minds of other humans. A nonreader lives his or her life, but a reader lives multiple lives.

On his walk that first night (fatal, in retrospect) he abruptly decided to take a look at the Spanish literature collection. He checked a floor plan posted near the stairwell, then climbed several flights to a floor that was entirely devoted to the world's languages and literatures. The Spanish part of it was colossal, easily several hundred thousand volumes. He wondered if any library in his own country could match such holdings. He was awed once again, but then grew angry. These gringos take everything! While the fools who govern us pay no heed to protecting and preserving our culture.

He picked up his pen to begin writing his talk. He would start with an epigram by Umberto Eco.

If God existed, he would be a library.

Can one sentence capture the essence of something that contains an infinite number of sentences? Umberto comes very close. Some would consider his epigram blasphemous, denying the existence of God while daring to describe the library as godlike. He privileges the divine attribute of omniscience. Infinite knowledge. An arrogant, Faustian claim, to be sure. Yet accurate as a description of the goal of the library.

Saved from hubris only because it is unattainable, because it is forever a work in progress.

In broadest terms, a library's mission is to collect, organize, preserve, and make accessible the recorded knowledge of mankind. To collect the best and exclude the rest. Treasure, not junk. Even a small library strives to do this by means of encyclopedias and reference works. A library says to mankind: Here is knowledge, here is quality, here is the lasting fruit of your labors, investigations, and art. Here is what everyone who came before you has discovered. A person who seeks knowledge, who wants to learn, can enter a library with the reasonable expectation that he or she will find it, or find some of it, immediately at hand. It is the starting point and eventually will be the ending point of research.

He set down his pen to avoid writing that the grandeur of the library thrilled him. Vast as a range of mountains, profound as the seas. Nature's mirror. And like nature even more absorbing when you get down on hands and knees to look at it: turning over leaf mold, capturing insects, taking samples of the soil. On his last trip to the United States, in Southern California, he spent a very pleasant afternoon at the Bowers Museum in Santa Ana, which has beautifully displayed holdings of Asian art among other delights. Of course, before leaving, he browsed in the

museum's bookstore. There he discovered an entire
wall of books on buddhism. Dictionaries, encyclopedias, editions of classic texts, scholarly tomes, poetry,
photographic essays, and a profusion of albums and
studies of buddhist art. All were brand new, in
perfect condition, exuding wonderful smells of
different inks and paper. The design and typography
of many volumes were exemplary, truly beautiful.
The hair on the back of his neck rose, and his scalp
began to tingle, and, deeper still, his mind. This is the
sort of thing you can never tell anyone or they'll
think you're crazy. He left that place of enchantment
with a stack of books under his arm, slightly dazed,
feeling like he had stolen fire from the gods.

Such a delicious experience, which, in a great
library, you can have over and over again.

THE MAIL CLERK dropped a pile of case files and
manila envelopes on the inspector's desk. One of
them, from the library, contained the list of missing
books. It was a computer printout about an inch
thick. He began to peruse it, recognizing a title now
and then, a couple of which he had actually read. He
looked for patterns and categories, but it was difficult. There were many subjects. Lots of the books

were quite popular, and likely just 'lifted' by curious or impatient patrons. Students often steal books. Setting aside probable petty thefts, he tried to focus on books of greater financial value. He guessed these would be older, often in literature or history, some in science, and especially accounts of explorations and voyages. He took note in particular of several titles that Señor Molina said he wanted to see, and did a double take when he spotted a title that he had long sought for his own collection—and finally found.

That did it. While he did not consider the case important, he decided he would pursue it. It would be a pleasant diversion from his regular duties.

That evening, when the inspector went home, he marched straight to his bookcase. He located the volume and discovered that it *was* the library's copy, stamped WITHDRAWN. He remembered he felt lucky at the time he bought it, and did not question why the library had disposed of such an interesting work. Perhaps they had another copy. For sure he would go by the bookstore and ask a few questions.

THE SHOP in question was in a lower-rent district. It was small, just one window in the front, and the books on display were dusty and faded. Inside the shelves were crammed, with overflow piled on the floor. It was more a used book store than a rare book store, though collectors did drop in because of occasional 'finds'. The owner smoked. He was old and dressed shabbily. His books smelled of tobacco. When you asked him a question, he looked at you for a moment through thick glasses, then gave a short answer, usually no. He didn't have it. Such stores are common in Latin American cities. They are where ordinary people go to buy books. In new books stores, as often as not, clerks are stationed at the entrance to intercept you to find out what you are looking for, and then follow you around. Many volumes will be tightly wrapped in cellophane. Leafing through them is generally not allowed. These stores can be large and beautiful, bright, clean, neat, with wonderful stocks arranged by subjects and then by authors A to Z. They are thrilling to true readers and candy to intellectuals. But only the well-off need enter, for the price of an ordinary book will be more than a day's pay.

When someone offers this man an unusual book or possibly a rare book, occasionally with ownership stamps still in it, he will stare at the person, he will stare and say nothing, then proffer a disappointing amount. The seller might be a schoolboy pilfering from his father's collection, a widow having to down-size to a smaller apartment, or a library employee.

Inspector Robles entered the shop, exchanged customary greetings, and began browsing. He quickly noticed a book he personally wanted to read, and placed it on the counter. Then continued browsing, selecting and examining numerous books, sometimes taking time to read a few paragraphs. Finally, ready to leave, he added two more books to his pile and slid them in front of the proprietor.

"I had some luck today."

"Good. Here's your receipt."

"NO DOUBT, HE'S THE FENCE." Inspector Robles was seated in Doctor Vidal's office. He placed three volumes on the desk. "I myself bought the first one from him two years ago, and the other two just yesterday. It's all quite brazen. No attempt has been made to disguise that the library owned these books. The ownership stamps are there. All he or the thieves did was mark them as withdrawn. It's common practice, isn't it, for libraries to weed their collections?"

"Not so often in Latin America. We fear little would be left. But you are quite right. All of these titles are on our list of missing books. And the one you found two years ago is a gem."

"Truly, I'm going to hate giving it back."

"Señor Robles, if I may ask, why are you interested in this book?"

"It's the first Spanish translation of *Le Père Goriot* by Balzac. I collect him, even in the original—which led me to study French. I learn so much about human nature from him. And of course I love his police stories. But enough about me. We need to devise a plan. First, tell me how libraries stop theft."

"They can't entirely, but here are some options. For inside jobs, search employees as they leave. Quite degrading, and, if determined, they could simply toss books out windows and retrieve them later."

"But shouldn't the windows be kept shut and locked?"

"In our climate? Without air-conditioning? In mid-Summer it would be stifling. We do already ask to look inside patrons' purses, briefcases, and back-packs as they leave. But there are a number of ways to circumvent such a cursory search. Thieves can modify a briefcase to create a secret pocket, hide material underneath their clothes, bring in a date stamp and ink pad to create a phony charge out, or worst of all, mutilate the book or the journal by cutting out the pages.

"Electronic security is common in North American libraries, but extremely expensive as well as labor intensive. Every volume in the collection has to be sensitized. And even this measure can be circumvented by a thief. He simply needs to locate and remove the magnetic strip hidden in the volume.

"Finally, there's the nuclear option: some of our North American colleagues eliminate the theft problem entirely by only offering e-books."

Detective Robles frowned. "Then I must go back to the old bookseller and lean hard until he gives up the names of the thieves."

"WHAT'S a sawhorse doing in the living room?"

"Oh! I'm going to have to chew out the carpenter. He's supposed to clean up everyday."

"What's going on?"

"I'm having some shelving put up in the guest room. Truth be told I haven't had a guest stay over in years, so I thought I might as well put the space to better use."

"How about me?"

"Teresa, when you stay over it's not in the guest room."

She smiled.

"So let's see."

They walked down the hall and into a room under construction. Three sawhorses, a ladder, tools, and a pile of lumber were on the floor. The bed, dresser, and other furniture had been removed. It was a nice room with light grey plastered stone walls, a saltillo tile floor, a fine wrought-iron chandelier, an adjoining bathroom, and at the far end arched windows and a glassed door opening to a private patio. She looked out the windows.

"Lovely."

Nearby were some cardboard boxes with a tarp covering them to keep sawdust off. She lifted a corner to peak, saw books, then pulled back the whole thing, and began reading titles:

"*Relación histórica del Viaje que hizo á los Reynos del Peru y Chile el Botánico Hipólito Ruiz en el año 1777 hasta el de 1788.*

Auguste de Saint-Hilaire, *Histoire des plantes les plus rémarquables du Brésil et du Paraguay.*

Richard Evans Schultes, *Ethnobotany: Evolution of a Discipline.*

What are you doing with these botany books? Is this a new interest?"

"Sort of . . . Philosophy, you know, is the mother of all subjects. A doctor of philosophy is licensed to study whatever he wants, wherever curiosity leads him. And, for that matter, so is a librarian. So on both counts . . ."

"Of course, *cariño*, now tell me the real reason."

"Did you know Professor Matteo Conti? The ethnobotanist. Probably not. He came and went before you were appointed. The university let him go after he became ill, too ill to teach. And he really didn't have a stable position, in spite of his standing as a scientist. He was a refugee, from Argentina, who fled the regime of General Jorge Videla. His appointment and re-appointments were always temporary, and included no benefits. Not a *centavo* for sick leave or retirement. So he was left in a bad way.

"We had become friends, so I tried to help him. Not much. A bag of groceries once in a while, a little money left on the entry table when I departed. Mainly just visiting. Being friends we had many good conversations. The reason we met in the first place was because he needed books, specialized books, which the university library and unfortunately our library lacked. He mentioned a few titles, some in print and some very old. They were mainly about indigenous food and medicinal plants. Knowledge from our own Indians. Original sources are found in accounts of early explorers—actually, before them, in pre-Columbian codices. Later came research by botanists and anthropologists. The literature is scattered all over the place.

"I began looking around for the titles Professor Conti needed. As I said a few were in print and I was able to buy them. And surprisingly I was able to find copies of several others in the antiquarian book market—but I couldn't afford any! I had no funds for these worthy books. This was not the first time I had felt such despair but it was the worst."

"Oh, Andrés, it's not your fault the library's budget stinks. You're at the bottom of the feeding chain. In this city, first we must pay our politicians, then the police. Not much is left over."

"*Exacto.* Consequently the library is a hodge-podge—depleted, worn out, and riddled with lacunae. There are no foci, no areas worth a researcher's attention. It's entirely hit and miss. Anyway, these were the books that were in my friend's apartment when he died. I brought them here."

"Do you read them?"

"Yes, I have started to take an interest in the subject."

"Why not give them to the library?"

"No, the library is not ready for such a collection."

"Really?"

"Enough. Too much shop talk. Let's eat. I have a

roast chicken in the refrigerator, some poached leeks, and a nice white wine."

Later, in a very comfortable mood, Teresa sipped the last drop of her wine, stretched languorously, and took his hand. "Come, *jardinero*, it's time for bed. I'm going to wind myself around you like a vine."

THE NEXT DAY was a very bad one for the old bookseller. A half-hour after he opened his shop Detective Robles and a uniformed policeman came through the door and took him into custody. They told him he was under investigation for receiving and fencing stolen public property. In addition the investigation would determine whether he was the actual thief of that property. In the interrogation room the three books the detective had personally purchased in the shop were spread across the table along with the receipt of purchase. The bookseller was informed that as they spoke other officers were searching the entire premises of his shop, including storage areas, and his home, to discover possible stolen property.

"Certainly our city library has been pillaged," snarled the detective, as he plunked down the thick list of missing books.

The bookseller, of course, claimed innocence. He

was a victim too, he said, since he believed the books had been duly withdrawn from the library. "Just look at the stamps."

"And just where and how did you obtain these supposedly withdrawn books?"

"The library discards books from time to time and tries to sell them at a cut rate. I buy a few."

"Wrong answer. As you can see, these books are in good condition and on important subjects. Not the kind the library discards."

"I don't know. That's what I remember."

"Careful, a faulty memory may implicate you as the thief as well as the fence, if we find no other links. Two serious charges, a double-whammy. Think about your position tonight while in your cell."

The next day the first thing the bookseller saw when he entered the interrogation room was a rubber stamp and ink pad in the middle of the table. The officers who had searched his shop the day before found them in a workbench drawer. The stamp read "WITHDRAWN".

"We have you, Señor Arenas. In court you will be convicted. The only thing left whereby you might help yourself is to cooperate. Cooperation can lead to leniency when you're sentenced. Are you interested?"

He lowered his head. "What do I have to do?"

"You need to tell us the extent of this illicit operation and who else was involved. By the way, in our search yesterday we found more stolen books. So we would like you to go through this list and mark those you have handled. Don't understate, or we won't believe you. Most of all we want you to tell us who the thieves were. It's them or you."

IT DIDN'T TAKE LONG. The bookseller accused two library employees of being the thieves. Both had worked there for years. They were shelvers, a low paid position. The three of them were now in custody, awaiting trial. The newspapers covered the arrests in considerable detail with photos. That was a desired outcome. The authorities hoped to scare off other would-be thieves.

As Detective Robles reported to Doctor Vidal, the defendants had collectively identified 320 books they had stolen over a five year period. "The real number is probably greater. Who knows? But I am glad we stopped this hemorrhage."

"Indeed. We are indebted to you for fine police work."

"Although it seemed too easy. I'm still bothered by some things."

"Like what?"

"Well, for one thing, no matter how hard we press them, our two suspects deny stealing any truly rare books. They claim those were out of their league, so to speak. It would make them too conspicuous. They wouldn't know where to safely sell them. In fact, none of the identified stolen property pertained to the books Señor Molina needed. The ones he wanted were very old. Colonial imprints, right? And all of a religious nature: Bibles, missals, catechisms, Church edicts, theology. He seems to be working on a history of Church dogma of that era. Is there much of a market for such books among collectors and libraries?"

"Well, yes and no—or rather I should say no and yes. Most active collectors would have almost no interest in the content of such works. There are tens of thousands of editions of the Bible. It is the most common book on earth. So they would be considered curiosities, except for their early date of publication. That fact gives them scholarly value in documenting the history and geography of printing. Still, the market's very limited. In the United States there are a select number of research libraries, mainly in the Ivy League, with so much money, with endowments so great, that librarians actually have to have regular brain storming sessions in order to figure out ways of spending it. I swear this is the truth, it comes from *a horse's mouth*, to use an English expression. (By the way, most libraries are not in such an enviable position, quite the contrary.) But in these libraries, in order to spend the money in an easy lazy way, they will develop some areas of the collection on the basis of automatic fill-in. In other words, anything they don't already have meeting certain criteria, they will buy. Colonial Latin American imprints are an example."

The detective was laughing. "I've never heard that expression, 'horse's mouth'."

"It is funny. In Spanish we would say *'Lo oí de buena fuente'*."

"Amigo, you are a riot. As for the case, baring new developments, it's closed. But I know we haven't solved it. Maybe we never will."

DOCTOR VIDAL RESUMED WRITING his lecture.

Let us imagine two buildings side by side. One is a library stuffed with books and the other a much smaller office building filled with computer terminals. The library isn't small but only has space to house a limited number of books. The office building, however, turns out to be a portal to the Digital

Archive of Everything Written. You may wonder what the difference is between these two institutions, other than size. Reduced to simplest terms, a library collects and organizes mankind's canons of knowledge while an archive like this just collects—everything—as its name implies. A library is quite selective in what it acquires, and then organizes its materials, mainly printed books, by means of cataloging rules and classification schemes. Books are grouped meaningfully, and new acquisitions are fitted into appropriate places among previous acquisitions. In an electronic archive items are given a unique, sequential accession number as they arrive, briefly cataloged, digitized, and then discarded. Most brief cataloging records will lack subject headings, so users have to rely upon key word searches to fish for appropriate materials. Quite hit or miss, just like the sport of fishing. A simple search might result in hundreds of thousands of hits, most of them wildly irrelevant and useless.

Thus, while an archive can be extremely useful if one knows exactly what one wants, if one searches for a specific author and title, this is often not the case, even for experts working outside of their immediate field. Remember, the archive we are imagining offers EVERYTHING, literally everything that has, is, and will be published. The good, the bad, porno . . . everything. All digitized. A hundred million e-books and counting. A bit much? We should never forget that the limitations of actual readers—who only live so long and who only read so fast and never fast enough—do not change. Man remains the measure. His practical problem in this case is epistemological: What should I read? Where should I begin? What book, what article? My time is limited.

In many respects the practice of librarianship is a continuous selection process, a narrowing of choices to just the texts a user needs. Quantity gives way to quality; relevance sharpens to pertinence. The search process does not begin in chaos, just anywhere, with everything. It begins in a carefully selected subset of everything. Thus the first job of librarians is to create the subset: to vet materials, draw the boundaries, and man the gateways. To perform the age-old task of winnowing the wheat from the chaff.

Please note that selectivity is not a disguise for censorship. Librarians loath censorship. Within any category of publications there is excellence and at the other end, junk. Gothic romance novels, bodice rippers, social science, cookbooks, celebrity biographies, mathematics, pornography, government publications, and so forth—any and all categories have their great examples and a vast amount of mediocrity. The librarian's job is to find and collect the best and exclude the rest.

At this point some of you in the audience might well exclaim: What incredible presumption these librarians have! Pretending to be the judge of what is known. Yet that is a fundamental function of librarianship, called subject bibliography. Every subject has a literature, which librarianship must know or have means of knowing. Librarians are not the authors of this literature, but rather assiduous students and curators of its bibliography.

As it stands now, a library is an institution offering the record of what is known and, ideally, nothing else. Not infallible and always a work in progress, but the best approximation to truth available. The gold standard.

But why not have access to both? you might ask. The library and the archive. It would be a reader's paradise and the ultimate scholar's workshop. I agree.

But this is not the way things are going. For those that hold the purse strings—governors, legislators, trustees, university presidents, and even many library directors—the digital archive is a dream come true. In their minds, it can replace libraries. No more buildings to fund, no more books to buy and shelve, no more librarians' salaries and pensions to pay, no more bottomless pit. And who can complain, the archive has everything.

Already, in North America, libraries are being re-named and re-purposed as community centers, featuring meeting rooms, exercise machines, yoga mats, even pool tables. The space allowed for books and quiet study keeps shrinking, and will ultimately be reduced to a room full of computer terminals.

More is at stake here than the demise of print. Concurrently, there is a demise in reading, indeed, in the ability to read. For the sake of argument allow me a gross generalization: that today's literate population may be divided into two broad groups: those who were taught to read using printed primers and children's books, and those who were taught to read using electronic devices. Unlike speaking, reading is not natural to the human being. It must be taught and practiced with increasingly difficult material for many years. Reading is a developmental skill which very significantly changes the physical makeup and operation of the brain. A new adult reader, who was previously illiterate, will be unable to read most adult fiction and nonfiction, let alone literary, schol-arly, or scientific texts. The cause is not a lack of intel-ligence but a lack of practice. His or her brain is not ready, not equipped, and may never be.

Even among digital devotees it is generally recognized that regular use of electronic devices results in a shortened attention span. This unfortunately...

Vidal put down his pen. He was getting too preachy and too technical. The audience would surely tune him out, if they had not already done so. He quickly jotted down a few notes, and called it a day.

REMAINING POINTS

A shortened attention span impedes fluent reading, reducing speed, comprehension, and interest in continuing.

Which leads to a strong preference for brief texts: a few sentences, a few paragraphs, a page or two. Anything longer is skimmed.

Long reads (articles, reports, books) are painful slogs.

It doesn't matter whether it's a print book or an e-book. Both are too long.

Ergo, the Digital Archive of Everything Written will hardly be used.

At a party he had attended in the U.S., an older woman, a librarian, stunned him when she said, "I'm tired of reading. I want the black box to tell me what the book says."

How he wished he had had the presence of mind

to say something clever. "A box is fine, but personally I'm going to hold out for a pill to swallow." Nonetheless her remark was unforgettable. She was the harbinger of post-literate society.

AFTER THE EVENING COOLED DOWN, they would have supper in the patio, a quiet, leafy refuge on the side of the house. If any wine was left they would carry it to a nearby sofa and relax, sharing gossip, memories, laughter, and playing with ideas . . . what ifs and fanciful hypotheses. Teresa especially enjoyed embroidering her trains of thought. She would sit up straight and begin talking with her hands. Andrés just watched, charmed. He liked her voice so much that sometimes he listened only to the sound. "Are you paying attention?" she would ask. That would rouse him, but it might lead to his reaching over and cupping her breasts. She would close her eyes and squirm, or cry out in mock modesty, "Unhand me, naughty boy! Let me finish my argument." He would relent and concentrate, until she talked too long, and became irresistible. Then his hand would slide under her skirt and up her thigh and into bliss. They were very happy. In her own home Teresa had bouts of insomnia. But in

his bed she curled around him and fell asleep in
minutes.

'WHAT A SURPRISE! So good to see you."

"*Hola, amigo.* I thought I would come by to see
how things are going."

"*Muy bien.* The library is peaceful."

"Any signs of new theft?"

"No, I believe we've scared off would-be perpe-
trators for the time being."

"Good. There is something else. During the investigation I became acquainted with a remarkable tool
you librarians keep to yourself. WorldCat. You, of
course, are familiar with it. For me, as a book lover, it
was a revelation. An on-line union catalog of 18,000
libraries around the world. Anyway, I was curious
about just how rare some of our missing volumes
were. I mean the old ones. So I looked up several
dozen entries, and found that a few were very rare
indeed. Copies of them were held by one, two, three,
four, no more than five libraries in the world.
Although I had closed the case, I decided out of
curiosity to keep track of the rarest titles, so once a
month I check WorldCat. Lo and behold, a university
library in the United States has just added two of

them to its collection. I find that very interesting. What do you think?"

"Absolutely."

"I thought you would agree, so I have asked an old friend of mine, an Interpol officer in the Cultural Crime Division, if he wouldn't mind contacting this university. He works out of New York, and he's quite willing to do us a favor. So we shall see."

"BINGO! This guy's been living in the U.S. for so long that he's picked up the slang. I didn't know at first what that word meant. But now I do."

Bingo! Your hunch was right. Plano University Library (a Texas up & comer) has your two stolen books. They had just recently been cataloged. The special collections librarian, who seemed very annoyed by my visit, retrieved them for me. They appeared to be in good condition, considering their age. I looked for property stamps, but all had been expertly removed. A forensic lab could probably reveal some traces. The librarian said the books had been legally purchased six months earlier from a known Latin American dealer. She produced the receipts. Price: $4,000 each. The dealer's name is

Miguel Osorio. Maybe you even know him, as he lives in your city! His address is a post office box (copy of receipt enclosed).

I told the librarian to keep the books safe and out of use pending repatriation. This annoyed her even more. She said she would be speaking with the university lawyers before anything like that happened. Then she gave me a little lecture about how the books were probably safer in her library than in yours (witness the theft). And if one takes a long view of civilization, they had finally found their home.

At this point I had to leave as I was getting ready to slug her.

Don't worry, amigo, international law is on your side, but I suppose justice could be delayed for years by the lawyers."

Saludos cordiales,

Juan Francisco Salazar

P.S. Next time we get together, you pay for the beer.

Detective Robles laid the letter on the desk. "Do you know this guy, Osorio?"

"Never heard of him."

"Nor is he listed in any city directory, including business licenses. How is it that our city has an unknown bookseller who, internationally, *is* known?"

"I'm dumbfounded. This is a lot worse than I thought."

"Any suspicions?"

"No."

"Well, I'm going to have this particular U.S. library payment traced through the banks. And maybe we'll find other payments. But it will take time. I'll keep you informed."

"VIDAL SPEAKING."

"*Hola*, Andrés, I don't have time to come by, but I wanted to let you know that the banks have been able to trace the checks to where they were cashed. Not only the Plano University checks, but two dozen others. All were cashed in Quito, where our bookseller has established a phony business identity under the same name. So far the amounts total $126,000."

"My god."

"Yes, we need to get this guy. If he tries to cash another check, he'll be apprehended. I've made arrangements."

"You were right when you said we have been

pillaged. I've been keeping the Director informed, of course, and we've decided, with a predator like this on the loose, that we must take immediate action to increase the security of the collection. So, we are conducting a shelf reading and inventory of the entire collection—getting books in proper order, determining for certain what's missing, and pulling all books published before 1875. These will be segregated into a separate collection. To make room for it, we are clearing out a large alcove, formerly a reading room, erecting shelving, and most importantly installing a strong iron cage barrier at the entrance. This will be our new rare book room. It should prevent further despoliation. We regret losing reading space—that hurts—but what else can we do?"

"May I ask why this wasn't done before?"

"Inertia, incompetence, lack of funds. A long-standing fiasco, in which I include myself."

Two Months Later

"WE'RE AT A STANDSTILL. No new checks have been cashed. I continue to monitor WorldCat but see no changes. We have no suspects. It looks like our bookseller has suspended business—at least temporarily."

"Perhaps because of all the publicity when the arrests were made. This guy isn't dumb."

"No, he isn't. I'm sure he's one our smartest citizens."

~

Five Years Later

DETECTIVE ROBLES SPREAD the newspaper across his desk and opened to the obituaries section. Yes, there was the announcement. Doctor Andrés Vidal.

He was only 63. No cause of death mentioned. Unmarried, no children. A senior library administrator for 35 years and adjunct university professor. Originally from the town of Girón, recognized early as an outstanding student, awarded scholarships to study abroad. B.A. from the University of North Carolina, Ph.D. from Duke.

Robles lowered his eyes and thought about his friend. They didn't see each other often, but had a bond. They had worked side by side. So sad. He felt quite alone.

A few days after the funeral, Detective Robles was contacted by Licenciado Nicolás Segura, a notary, who said he was handling the deceased's estate. He said that Doctor Vidal in his will had left the detective a letter, which was to be found on his desk at home. "He expressed hope that you could pick it up in person, which is the reason for my call. Could we arrange, at your convenience, a visit to the property?"

A couple of days later they met at the front door. The house was a single-story, old colonial, solidly built, handsome, the work of master carpenters and masons. Inside it was cool and subdued, a very comfortable place, with art and nice furnishings.

"Doctor Vidal wanted you to have time to read this letter in private. He said you were the most trustworthy man he had ever known. So I am going to take leave and attend to other business. All you have to do when you depart is lock the door. Good day. It was a pleasure meeting you."

For a few minutes Detective Robles wandered around the living room and adjacent dining area and peaked into the kitchen, which was neat and clean. Through a window above the sink he could see part of the patio and garden. Then he returned to the desk, sat down, switched on the lamp, and opened the envelope. It contained a typed letter of many pages and a key.

My Dear Friend,

I had long hoped to express the contents of this letter to you personally. I imagined doing so after a fine dinner, served with my best wines. A night of good conversation. I even planned the menu. However, the more I thought about it, the more I feared it might lead to a possible misunderstanding, even a falling out. I did not want that to happen.

When Teresa died, so unexpectedly, of a brain aneurism, my life effectively ended. I have been operating on auto-pilot, doing everything by the numbers. Now my doctor informs me that I will soon join her. Believe me, I am ready.

This will be a long letter, and some parts of it will undoubtedly puzzle you. Please bear with me. Everything will be explained.

Let's begin by talking about Aimé Bonpland. Two hundred and twenty years ago two healthy, ebullient, brilliant young men in their twenties began a scientific expedition to Latin America, which, five years later, would dramatically expand mankind's knowledge of the world. They were, of course, Alexander von Humboldt and Aimé Bonpland. Bonpland is not nearly as well known as Humboldt, but he was co-equal in the expedition. He had previously studied medicine and botany in

Paris. His teachers were the finest in France, great scientists like Jean-Baptiste Lamarck and Antoine Laurent de Jussieu. Bonpland loved studying plants. In field work he was passionate, tenacious, and skillful. During the expedition he took serious risks to obtain specimens. And with what results! Altogether, he and Humboldt brought back 60,000 plant specimens, of which 6,000 were new species.

Their expedition was just the beginning of a fabulous life which I cannot relate in this letter. Bonpland spent the next 14 years in France, mainly as director of gardens for the Empress Josephine. But he often daydreamed about returning to Latin America, a more insouciant and *simpático* land, where he could continue his pursuits as a naturalist. He was already great friends with Simón Bolívar, having first met him in Paris' finest brothel. And another revolutionary, later to become Argentina's first president, Bernardino Rivadavia, invited him to emigrate to Buenos Aires to become a professor of medicine at the university and the founding director of the natural history museum. So he did, leaving Europe for good in 1817, accompanied by a young wife, her daughter, 500 citrus trees, many plants, and countless seeds. His shipboard nursery proved providential for the promised appointments came to nothing due to political turmoil. For the next three years he made his living selling fruits and vegetables. Then abruptly he leaves his wife, going up river 800 kilometers to Corrientes and onward to Misiones in Paraguay. Perhaps the words I use are too harsh, for with so much deteriorating and spinning out of control in Buenos Aires (financially, academically, socially) Bonpland was desperate to resume serious botanizing and possibly make a fortune. Circumstances permitting, the family might have a chance to reunite.

Uppermost in Bonpland's mind, not surprisingly, was a plant: *yerba mate*. The green tea brewed from it was the beverage of choice in the Southern Cone. It had immense economic value. At the same time it was a botanical mystery. The Guaraní Indians had long harvested leaves from this wild and uncommon tree, the *Ilex paraguariensis*. The Jesuits, observing them, successfully cultivated it at their utopia in Misiones. But how they did so was a secret, a lost secret. It was almost impossible to grow from seed. That is, until our genius, Bonpland, observed on the river island Martín García, birds eating the seeds, and grasped at once that *yerba mate* was one of those unusual plants that sprout only after passing through the intestines of an animal. With this knowledge he too could devise means of cultivating it.

So he settled amidst the Jesuit ruins in Misiones, and began his plantation. Unfortunately the land was in disputed territory, also claimed by Paraguay. And the fact that he was growing *yerba mate*, a Paraguayan state monopoly, enraged its dictator, José Gaspar Rodríguez de Francia, who promptly ordered 400 troops to cross the Paraná River, destroy the buildings, kill the workers, and capture Bonpland. For the next nine years he would be Francia's prisoner. Placed under house arrest in a village, he was forbidden to travel or correspond with anyone. Spies watched him and soldiers were nearby. To live he could practice medicine and farm. Bonpland, as usual, made the most of it and eventually prospered. He even married the daughter of a Guaraní cacique and had two children.

For another 29 years Bonpland would live through numerous adventures and close calls and never stop botanizing and learning. But I am going to end the sketch here, when he married María, the Indian girl.

What I am going to say next would be inappropriate in a scholarly article because evidence supporting it is scarce and scattered, though not contradictory. It is based on a hunch. I'm sure that you as a police detective often follow your hunches, and so, as an intellectual historian and book collector, must I.

During his long life of 84 years, Bonpland chased and loved countless women, married some (without divorcing any), and fathered lots of children. Does this make him a Casanova? I don't think so. His portraits, most executed when he was older, show a man of average appearance, certainly not handsome nor dressed in finery. Not a trace of *donjuanismo*. What does come through are penetratingly observant eyes. Sometimes they fell upon a plant, sometimes a woman. Interestingly, the plant he most loved to collect was an orchid because it reminded him of a woman's vagina— and South America is full of orchids. What's more, women loved him back, desired him, trusted him —no matter whether they were French, Spanish, Creole, Mestizo, or Indian. No doubt as a medical doctor he knew how to give women great pleasure. And of course he would want to.

Indians also trusted him. For many, especially in the jungle, Humboldt and Bonpland were their first contact with Europeans—and not the usual sort. They came to learn, not instruct, not exploit, not convert nor conquer. We can be sure the

Indians observed these two white men as closely as they were being observed, and apparently concluded that they were not deceitful nor hostile, just eager to learn everything they could about nature. As barriers fell, the Indians proved very generous, sharing their great knowledge. Above all, Bonpland, as a doctor, had interest in medicinal plants, and he witnessed many treatments employing them. Later, in his own practice, often in remote regions, he had difficulty reordering European medicines. Yet people kept coming to him for help. So he employed indigenous remedies —and why not? They often worked. One time a poisonous snake bit a farm worker when he stuck his hand inside some foliage. He ran to Bonpland, who applied an herbal poultice, which was all he had. Four hours later the man's condition had grown far worse, so he transported him by cart to a nearby Indian village where their medicine man, using a different *materia medica*, cured him. This was the kind of thing Bonpland registered in notebooks, plant descriptions, and botanical catalogs. However, a great many of his documents never survived the tropics. Insects, rodents, heat, humidity, mildew, canoes swamped in turbulent rivers, unretrieved luggage, military actions, thefts, and even a shipwreck on way to Europe took their toll. And in what concerns us, a very important document, which did survive, disappeared.

This document was a compendium describing 5,000 tropical and subtropical plants, the product of 45 years of botanizing and observation: a manuscript known as *La Nomenclature de Bonpland*. It circulated among a small group of Argentine scientists in the late 19th century, and one Brazilian who examined it claimed that it was the fundamental record of Bonpland's astonishing knowledge of indigenous medicine. The fount, one might say, for future research. Let us remember that Darwin himself called Bonpland "the best of judges." Unfortunately, the last person to borrow the manuscript never returned it.

You see I could talk on and on about the interesting Monsieur Bonpland, but now we must turn our attention to another person: Professor Matteo Conti. He was an ethnobotanist at our university and before that at the University of Buenos Aires. He had to flee Argentina when the Videla regime took over and began hunting intellectuals. We met because he needed advice and help in obtaining certain botanical books, which neither the university library nor ours had. I was able to find quite a few of them, which, when they weren't too expensive, he purchased and added to his personal collection. He was very affable, and we became friends. Eventually his health failed, interfering with his teaching, and the university laid him off. His position had always been tenuous. He was too sick to do field work, but he still published articles derived from analysis and reflection of printed sources. His own collection of books kept him going.

That collection he bequeathed to me upon death. A lot of books, a small suitcase, a letter, and a key. I hauled everything over to my house as there was no other place to put it. The contents of the letter shocked me, for he said the suitcase contained a treasure. He gave no indication of how he had come by this treasure, only that he felt compelled to remove it from Argentina, given that murderous barbarians were in power.

I took the key and opened the suitcase. Inside were four thick neatly-wrapped parcels. I carried them to a table and unwrapped the first parcel. It was a handwritten manuscript bound in boards. The title page read *La Nomenclature des Plantes Tropicales d'Amérique*, Vol. I, Aimé Bonpland.

I was stunned. I stood up and walked around the room, then walked out into the garden. There was no question, it was a treasure. A unique, unpublished work of the first order, of immense untapped scientific value, as well as extreme monetary value. For a librarian or a book collector to hold such a work in his hands, and indeed possess it, is a culminating moment of life.

The manuscript, after Bonpland's death, had never had a home. As far as we know, it had not belonged to anyone or any institution. It circulated, and had been missing for more than 100 years. And now I had custody of it, but I really didn't feel I owned it. Mankind owns such works.

I spent the next few weeks reading the entire thing. It was sometimes difficult deciphering his handwriting, which was small, even scribbled. Diligent editing will be needed in order to publish it, but that is not my job. Overall it was legible. A nomenclature systematically classifies a subject, so entries were grouped in plant families. They varied in length from a line or two to long paragraphs. A typical entry might include the binomial scientific name (if established), the common name in Spanish or Portuguese, the indigenous name (mostly Guaraní, which Bonpland spoke), a description of the plant, habitat, and known uses. Food and medicinal plants were always identified, with, in the latter case, the disease named and how the remedy was prepared and applied. Of course, not all entries were so complete.

For a very long time I puzzled over what to do. My mind went everywhere, but eventually options fell into two categories. I could sell it or donate it. It was worth a lot of money. At Christie's in London or Sotheby's in New York or the Hôtel Drouot in Paris numerous institutions would bid for it, and a case could be made why some of them were fitting destinations (for example, Le Jardin des Plantes, which already had many of Bonpland's papers and specimens). Of course, ultimately, the manuscript would go to the highest bidder. Let's say Harvard got it.

As a South American this stuck in my throat. Why should this fundamental research about our land, our plants, our indigenous people wind up in a foreign country? Why should we lose this key to future scientific work? This opportunity, so appropriate? I decided not to sell.

Donation, on the other hand, had its own problems.

Number One: "Casting pearls before swine." A donation to most academic institutions would likely proceed as follows:

Publicity

A ceremony upon receipt

Exhibit in library lobby

Deposit in special collections department

Indeed the manuscript might just be left in the lobby's glass case, in effect becoming a show piece, a museum object, a fossil.

I pondered this scenario for a long time before formulating a different plan, one that would compel a worthier destiny for my Bonpland. As great as the manuscript was, it nonetheless lacked sufficient critical mass by itself to provoke institutional adaptation and growth. The way forward was to see it as a lodestone, powerfully attractive. As a librarian it was obvious to me that it could become the cornerstone of a major research collection. Indeed, Professor Conti had already begun laying the foundation with his personal collection. It was my task to continue the process and build this library. So, with my own money, my own salary, I started buying books on ethnobotany in Spanish, French, Portuguese, English, and German. It's something I know how to do. However . . .

Problem Number Two: Some books were just too expensive—and they were highly desirable. This is when I turned rogue. Now I'm confessing to you, Guillermo. You can finally solve the case. Yes, to shine the worst light on it, I began using the public library as a piggy bank. I tried to pick a subject I thought almost no one was interested in, to do the least damage and to avoid detection. *Church history*. But, as you know, I was wrong, I miscalculated. Señor Molina was passionate about it.

So yes, I became the mysterious bookseller Osorio. *El Librero*. Turned out I was good at that too. I amassed tens of thousands of dollars for my special acquisitions fund. Mind you, I never spent a penny on myself. It all went into the books. Ahh, what books! My friend (I hope I can still call you that), just walk down the hall to the first door on the right. Inside you will find an outstanding specialized library on ethnobotany ready for use. A veritable force field. The manuscript is in the locked case built into the bookshelves. You have the key. In addition, when my home is sold, the proceeds will turn into an endowment to support this library in perpetuity. I am offering this package to our own university, provided they establish an Aimé Bonpland Center for Ethnobotanical Research. If they don't, it goes somewhere else.

So there it is.

Que te vaya bien!

Adiós,

Andrés Vidal

For a moment Detective Robles stared into space.

Then he chuckled and soon was roaring with laughter. "Andrés my friend, you are completely loco, but nobly so. How you try me! You who should be tried. For theft and bibliomania. What did Balzac say? 'The secret of great fortunes without apparent cause is a crime forgotten, for it was properly done.' Like yours. *Híjole!* What a choice. I suppose at this late date there's no reason to disturb the plan."

Detective Robles folded the letter and placed it in his coat pocket. Then walked home.

ABOUT THE AUTHOR

Peter Briscoe has had the pleasure not only of living with books as a reader but also of making them his life's work as a librarian and writer. For more than 30 years he built library collections at two universities. A specialist in collection development, book acquisitions, special collections, and preservation, he directed efforts that led to the purchase or donation of 1.5 million volumes from all over the world on nearly all subjects. He loved his job but increasingly worried about the fate of books and reading in a digital, post-literate world. Briscoe is Associate University Librarian Emeritus at the University of California, Riverside. He is the author or co-author of five books, including a translation from the French of José Cabanis' novel *Night Games* (1993), *Reading the Map of Knowledge* (2001), *The Best-Read Man in France* (2012), and *Mexico at the Hour of Combat* (2012).

www.peterbriscoebooks.com

CPSIA information can be obtained
at www.ICGtesting.com
Printed in the USA
FSHW011135230121
77931FS